SHADES OF LOVE

(Love comes in different forms and shades)

By

Rhoda Harika

FanatiXx Publication
AM/56, Basanti Colony, Rourkela 769012, Odisha
ISO 9001:2015 CERTIFIED
Website: www.fanatixx.in

© **Copyright, 2019,** RHODA HARIKA

"SHADES OF LOVE "
By: RHODA HARIKA
ISBN: 978-93-89106-86-2
Anthology of Hindi Write-ups 1st Edition

Book Formatting: Hemant Bansal | **Cover Design:** Sagar Samal

Contents

Dedication:

My parents and family members for recognising my passion and supporting me throughout my journey of writing.

My Late Grandmother, Mrs Santoshamma Kilari for all her prayers and blessings to make my dreams come true.

Acknowledgements

I would like to thank my parents, Dr M. Venu Gopal Rao and Dr M Babita Jain for always supporting me to follow my passion. My family members for standing by my side throughout my journey of writing this book.

I would also thank my friends, Sadaf, Swati, Smita, Shristy and Praful who encouraged me throughout the time when I thought of giving up. And my writer's family, family by choice, Dev sir, Nandhini ma'am, Renesa, Ankush and Atanu for being my support system and inspiring me to complete this book.

About the Author

Rhoda Harika is a proud Indian girl born in a South Indian family. She is basically from Visakhapatnam, the port city of Andhra Pradesh, the sunrise state of India. She completed her graduation in computer science engineering from Raipur Institute of Technology, Raipur, Chattisgarh. She was always passionate about writing and loved poetry. Right from her school days, her poems were published in newspapers and this encouraged her to improve her skills of writing and poetry. When she was in her college, she started a page on Instagram with id "lostgirl_from_heartstrings". Within a few days, her works were recognised and she was approached for many anthologies. She worked in anthologies such as, "THAT INDIAN GIRL" by Devesh Jaiswal, "UNHEARD WORDS OF SOUL" by Khushbu Gadiya, "FOIANS", "JE TAIME", "KHITAAB", and VAJRA World Record Holder "MAPLES" by Shreya Kanodia, "MISERY OF WORLD", by Japneet Kaur, "KHWABO KI AATISH", by Sudhi and Abhay Singh and "MUBADARA" by Bismita Acharya

HOW I FELL IN LOVE WITH MY BEST FRIEND

INTRODUCTION

It was a bright Sunday morning. It was A BIG DAY for me, and I was standing in front of the mirror staring at myself. Dressed in a white long lace gown, with a veil pinned to my brown bun, and holding a bunch of roses in my hand, I walk towards the window, and when I peep out, I saw him, Jay, he looks so stunning in this tuxedo thing, I remember him saying tuxedo isn't his thing but now, he is in one for me. I wonder how long we have come across from the day we met to this day.

Chapter 1: How We Met

Hi! My name is Kia, am a fair toned girl with black wavy hair. And Jay is my best friend. He is a tall handsome guy always with a spark in his eyes. We met when we were five when jay's family moved back to south India. Jay's grandparents were south but his father moved to the north to expand their business. Once their branch at the north was settled, they handed it over to jay's uncle and moved back to the south to live with jay's grandparents.

Jay's house was just two blocks away from mine. We live on the same street and study in the same school. When I was five, I was a cry baby. Seriously, even when I couldn't' find my pencil, I would shed tears. One day during our lunch in school, I was running to the ground and I slipped on the stairs and got rolled down to the ground floor. Though it was a super fast way to reach the ground, I bruised my knees and started crying, like a crying baby. It was then when he first spoke to me. He was there hiding behind those stairs playing hide and seek with his friends. When he saw me crying, he came for my help. I still remember his first words;" don't cry like a baby, you are a grown-up girl now. You started schooling and you're still crying?", that was so embarrassing, I felt angry that he reacted in such a pathetic way. Before I could reply, his friends came in and he was caught as he was hiding no more. The school bell rang and we all rushed back to our classes.

Later that evening, he came to a garden in our locality, where I was sitting on a swing and he enquired about my knee. This was a friendly gesture. We were just starting to have a conversation when some kids of our age maybe 7 or 8 came to us and started bullying. They wanted me to get out of that swing as they want to play on it. They made fun of my height that I was too short and my legs don't reach the ground when I am on a swing and I should better play with sand building some castles or something. We were forced to move away from that place. So, we went off to sand tub over the other side of the garden.

I sat in the sand tub and started shoving it with and filling the sand bucket but I don't remember what I really was up to. Jay was standing there without uttering a word and with a sharp gaze on those bullies. Suddenly he caught me by my hand and started walking. I followed in wonder what was happening and tried to ask him, "where are we going?". He gave a stern look and I shut my mouth. We went to his home and there he showed me a long inverted u-kind of thing with two handles above and a ladder on one side and slide on another. He asked me to climb up the ladder, hold on to those handles and hang in the air. He said his father told him that this would increase his height and he doesn't want people to call me a dwarf. Every day after school he would pull me in here and make me do this.

At first, I hated him but slowly we become best friends. Time flew and our friendship got thicker with time. We sit in school bus together, then on the same bench in class, eat lunch together, get back home together, play and study together. Our bond of friendship brought our families close and now our parents turned to close friends too. Life was all good. He would help me in sports and I would teach him for exams. We were like complete, my flaws were his perfection and his flaws were mine. Then we grew up so fast, we had left with only memories and count of days. We were happy sharing notes, fighting for chocolates and blamed each other for our mistakes. We were unaware of what the future holds for us.

Chapter 2: Jay's First Love

We have entered our teens. Teenage, the age of love, misunderstandings, jealousy, friendship, frustration and fun. We got promoted to 9th grade. As per our school policies, no more new admissions for after class 9. This was the last year for students who want to transfer in and out of our school.

Everyone was sitting outside the class near the gallery, looking out for new admissions. The school bell rang and everyone got back to their classes. In our class, we did meet some new faces but none were so interesting. It was the first period, the math class by Ms Malini. She was teaching Algebra. Then there was a sudden knock on the door and a girl called out," please, may I come in ma'am?". When Ms Malini called her in, she entered the class, introduced herself as 'Lisa'. Then she scanned for an empty place and sat on the bench beside mine.

She was fair, with long beautiful tresses and not to mention a beautiful face cut along with the perfect height for her body. Her eyes, they were so clear like crystals and her smile so wide and attractive. Before you conclude I was checking her out, let me clear that every boy in our class was describing her. And jay, he has already swapped his place with mine, to have a seat next to her. I think Jay kinda liked this new girl.

It was about a week that Lisa has joined our class and since then Jay was busy impressing her and now we rarely talk. Sometimes, though we three hang out together, there is nothing like before. After a few more days, they announced that they are in love with each other. Am seriously happy for Jay, but what hurts me is that even after being his best friend, I came to know this from their friends' book status. That evening I went to Jay's house after dinner. I thought of giving him a nice tight slap and then ask what's wrong with him. But I never thought things will turn out this way...

Chapter 3: Who is Karan?

That night as I had already thought, I went off to Jay's house after my dinner. To my surprise, Lisa was already there. They were having dinner together. When they saw me there, they were surprised. But things didn't turn out much worse. Thanks to Jay's mom, who raised a conversation about my friendship with Jay and how we used to hang out together all the time. After some chit chat, when aunt left us three in a room. As I was about to leave for home, Lisa stopped me. She said now she understands how would have been feeling all this time, away from your best friend and maybe lonely too. Both of them were sorry for not spending time with me. That night things changed completely. Now it's we three who hang out every time. Though I sometimes come up with stupid excuses and give them some private couple time, yet it's fun to be together. Now I have my best friend and a new good friend to hang out with and have fun. That weekend we planned a trip to a nearby camping site. So, we were all busy packing things, completing assignments and stuff throughout the week.

And finally, the weekend has arrived. Jay rented a car and we both drove to pick Lisa on the way. When we reached Lisa's place, Lisa was there standing with a boy. When we stopped the car, she got in and introduced that boy as her childhood friend 'Karan' and asked her whether he could join us too. Karan was cute, tall and well built. I replied, "yes, of course". I was just thinking I can leave the love birds some private time and not get bored alone. I was just hoping for some company. Let's wait for this trip to unveil.

Chapter 4: Let's go Camping

It took us about an hour to reach the camping spot and another hour to find a good place and set up the tents. Lisa and I shared a tent while the boys were sharing the other. After taking some rest, we made some food and sat there having some talks and playing games. It was right before we were about to leave when Karan asked for my number. We exchanged numbers and bid goodbyes. By the time, we reach home, it was too late. So, I dozed off immediately. The very next morning, I woke up to a good morning text from Karan. I replied back to the good morning text and went off to school. All I could think about was Karan all day. There was something about him that made me think about him again and again. I couldn't concentrate much on the class. When in the evening I went back home, I got a call from him asking,"' can we meet again? Just you and me?". It was a little surprising but I said," you live in another city and you came yesterday only to meet Lisa and how will we meet again?" for which he replied," if you are willing to meet, I could come all this far again but just for you". Thus our date was fixed for the other day for he has to attend school back after tomorrow. Though I don't know whether to call it just a meet-up or some date. Whatever it is I was asked not to let Jay know about this.

The other day I made up an excuse for jay and left to meet Karan. He got some flowers for me and when I reached near him, he gifted them to me. Aaawww! Kinda romantic right. Then we went to a movie. It was a rom-com movie and I could feel him watching me throughout the movie. After that movie, we walked into a restaurant nearby to have some food. When we had food, he suddenly went to the manager and said something in his ear and came back. After a few minutes, there was some music put on and then suddenly he kneeled down with a rose in hand and OMG, he proposed me. Just before I could say anything, Jay and Lisa were here. Jay took me by my hand and rushed me into his car and we drove back home. Lisa and Karan were left in the restaurant and jay didn't even bother to tell Lisa a word. She looked upset when we were leaving or should I say when I was forcibly pulled to leave.

While at home, Jay was looking angry. He pulled me to his room and shouted what was wrong with me. I replied, "what is wrong with you? What do you think you were doing in there?". He shouted at me," what were you doing with Karan and what was he doing on his knees? Don't you think you should let me know about this or anything?". I lost my temper and replied, "what do you mean by what he was doing, he proposed to me and just before I could answer you brought me down here?". And the fight continued for a couple of moments when I left the room in anger. I went back to my home and locked myself in my room and cried to sleep.

Chapter 5: Breakup

We both stopped talking to each other after that night. It was past a few months now. We got promoted to class 10. We were both in our own lives. He was dating Lisa and I was with Karan. But losing a best friend affected our lives a lot. We both got short-tempered and within a few months, we both had heartbreaks. Karan broke up with me right after Lisa broke up with Jay. now we both stay all alone, no best friend and no love.

Ms Malini, our maths teacher is my favourite. She is so good to be true but everyone in the class, sorry in our school loves her a lot. She looks perfect. She is tall and not so skinny and her curly black locks, oh man! I myself love them. And then she carries herself so gracefully and her voice so sweet. Isn't this weird, how can someone be so perfect?

She had been noticing what was happening between me and jay. She was the only teacher in school, who saw us and our bond from class 1 and referred us as a role model to all others. But when all this happened to us, she was also as depressed

and worried as we were. One day she called me and Jay after school, to her home. She showed us an album. It was full of our pictures. Yes, me and jay and some other friends too. She told us that she had a friend when she was young and they shared a bond like us too. We always reminded her of that friend. She showed us how in our pictures, other friends did change, but we were always together and asked us to sit and sort things before its too late. She made us some tea and cookies while we sat there in silence looking at that album. Suddenly we found another album under the table where this was placed. I opened that to find some more pictures but to my surprise, it had pictures of a girl and a boy like me and jay. But the girl looked a bit familiar and after flipping more pages, I recognised it was Ms Malini and the other person must be her best friend as she mentioned. Then we kept on flipping pages, watching their pictures at different locations and in different poses when we came across her wedding photo. She was married to her best friend? This made both of us little awkward but then she came out with tea and I immediately placed back the album back in its place. After having tea, we head back home and this time, for the first time in our lives in complete silence but still together. We cried all the way home and finally

when we reached home, we said sorry to each other and hugged and promised never ever to fight again. At that moment we didn't know, that we would break that promise that soon.

Chapter 6: Bidding Farewell

After meeting Ms Malini that day, everything went back to normal between me and jay. Finally, the time has come for farewell. Now, we are about to complete our schooling and enter into junior colleges for 11th and 12th. Farewell was the last school function we all will be attending together. Everyone has different dreams in mind and all of us will be moving to different places and different fields. This is so emotional, am gonna miss all of them. "This day I will enjoy my fullest and make memories that would last forever", with such thoughts in mind,I got ready for the farewell function. I borrowed my mom's saree and jewellery for today's party.

That day at school, all class 10th girls were in sarees and boys were in suits. Everyone is suddenly looking like grownups. We have some events, cultural programs followed by speeches and a lavish lunch. Then we had some photoshoot sessions with teachers and friends. That evening after school, we had another non-formal Party. This was organised by all of our classmates and was at a nearby cafe in our locality. Since we didn't get much time to change, we were in the same traditional attire. That day I received many compliments on my looks. 'I was looking beautiful in saree', that was what everyone was saying. After the party, we were about to drive back home when I noticed something different. Jay was waiting for me at the parking lot. He had a rose in hand and the moment I went near, he played music in the car and proposed me. At first, I was taken aback but then when he mentioned that "our past relations didn't work because we were destined to be together, even Ms Malini married her best friend. We did see in her album, right? Then why not us?" I didn't have an answer but I knew I liked him too and maybe he was right, we are made for each other. I said "yes" and hugged him tightly blushing. We danced together for a while and went to our houses.

The next day in the morning, we went to school as usual. But this time there was something different in our behaviour, we both were too happy to be normal. Some or other actions of ours would make people around us give suspicious looks. And this continued for some days. Then we had our board exams and we both got busy preparing for exams and giving our exams.

Chapter 7: College Life

It was over a month. Our exams got over and our families planned for an outing together. It was more like a picnic. Dads were playing golf, moms were making snacks and gossiping and we both had enough privacy to wink and smile every now and then between our normal conversations. Then after some food and play, our parents called us for something important. They made us sit with them and made this announcement that "Jay's dad had got transferred to Bangalore. They have to move within a week". This made my heart feel so heavy and tears rushed down my cheeks. Everything was just going well. It was just yesterday when he proposed and we made promises for forever and now? Why does he have to leave? Why did uncle get transferred? Thoughts weren't just came running to my mind. They crashed and bumped into each other in my head. This was super painful than expected. To watch them pack things, to watch them book tickets and to watch them leave. Within no time, the week was over and they were already leaving. Before an hour or so, they were about to leave, we had a silent conversation. We just kept looking into each other's eyes and kept shedding tears. We again promised to talk on the phone at least for once a day and pay a visit to each others place for every holiday. And jay left for Bangalore with his family.

Days passed and we got busy in our school schedules, and just a phone call a day. I got elected as creative head of our student council and he was nominated for presidentship in Bangalore. We would have late night conversations for only a few minutes and then either of us would sleep over the phone after such a busy schedule. For every holiday declared at college, either jay would come down here or I would go over there. Everything was happy and happening until… until we transferred to the same college.

Yes, after successful completion of our junior college, we both planned and applied at a college in Indore. We both took engineering but choose different branches. Jay opted for civil while I was interested in computer science. We stayed at the college hostels. Boys hostel was on the college campus but our girl's hostel was near the head office of our college. The first year was fun making friends and sitting in the same class together. It was the second year when we were sent to respective branch buildings accordingly. At first, we would meet after classes and during lunches and on Sunday outings. But as our seniority increased, responsibilities and so did make a distance between us. We don't get enough time together now. We have extra classes after college and some activity club shopping or fest preparations or assignments on Sundays. We study in the same college, but even looking at each other has been a tough thing for us. He was busy bagging prizes in sports and me in academics. He has off-campus field trips while I attend on-campus coding challenges. Without any official announcement, we both unknowingly broke off our relationship, but deep down in hearts, we were still together.

Chapter 8: The End

And suddenly, I felt a tap on my shoulder. I shrieked in surprise to find 'Myra', Jay's wife. After Jay and I called off our relationship, we didn't fight like kids but stayed together like before. After some time, when after graduation, Jay started working, he met 'Myra'. They both fell in love and when their parents accepted their love, they tied knots together. I found my love in my father's choice ' Ryan '.

"If you are all ready, let's go Kia", Myra said. And with a deep breath, I walk holding flowers in hand and down the stairs. As I stepped down the last stair, I trembled and was about to fall when Jay came for my help. This gown is so beautiful but I am not yet used to carry it around. "Cant you even walk by yourself?" saying so again he made fun of me. But he walked me to the entrance where my dad took my hand and walked me through the aisle as the tradition says. I see people, my relatives and friends stand there and watch me walk towards the aisle. There was Ms Malini too with her husband Malik and kids. Then I made "I do" vows with Ryan on my "The Big Day".

It was then when we (Jay and Me) realised that we weren't made for each other. We are not for that "marriages are made in heaven" material. We were meant to be together forever as "best friends". Best friends who share love, care and happiness and pain. Best friends who fight all day but at the end of the day, who stand for each other. Best friends who love each other more than any lover in the world. And best friends like Kia and Jay.

Not every best friend are made to be Malini-Malik. Nor even everyone is made to be Kia-Jay. Some Malini's are made for Malik's and some Kia's for Jay's. Everyone has a different story to lead and different destiny to proceed.

28

SMILES AND LOVE

INTRODUCTION

It was my first day at work. After a formal introduction, I was told to be seated at my place and begin with the basics. The day was quite calm until it was noon. After lunch, a few people from my office from different sectors gathered to form a group and were having some chit chat. Then suddenly when I heard them laughing I looked back, and then at that moment, I saw a smile. It caught my attention. I still remember how that smile was, kind of energetic and true. With an attempt to have a look at that smile's owner, I lean a bit forward and finally caught sight of him. To be honest, he wasn't too handsome to lose my heart at first sight but he sure does have that cute smile that can make one's heart flutter. For a minute or so I lost in his smile to realise I should look away before he catches me staring at him and as I was thinking all this, our eyes met. I just looked away immediately and continued to work as nothing has happened at all.

The next day at lunch, we met. Not in a proper manner, but came to know his name when his friends were calling out to him. I kept on waiting for the moment, he would smile and I could have a glimpse at that smile. All the while we were having lunch, I would never miss a moment to have a glimpse of his smile without him noticing me. All my day I wait for him to come anywhere near my desk just to have a look at his smile. Making pretty sure not being caught by any. I don't name this love cause maybe this is just a simple attraction towards his smile. This may seem weird about a girl praising for a boy's smile but there is some magic in his smile, that whenever I see him smile, it brings a smile on my face.

Days started passing by. With me secretly admiring his smile and his unknowingly smiling around with his gang. Now every morning I wake up to doll up and look presentable. Maybe I am trying to make a good impression. I like the way this is happening. No talks, no gestures, no conversation, just me alone secretly admiring his smile. It past few weeks and I had some mutual friends of his added to my friend's book account but not him. Every time I see his name on the suggestions bar, my cursor just stays there, kind of stuck on the 'send' button but doesn't dare enough to click on it. Gradually I started waiting for him to come around and to secretly catch a glimpse. Every time our room door is opened, I find my eyes glued on the door in search of him.

One fine day, when I was at work and was just checking my friend's book, his name popped up again in the suggestions bar and this time, I thought of giving a try and ended up clicking on the 'send' button. The moment the request was sent, I started feeling anxious. I was all tensed up thinking about the response and after an hour or so, I got a positive response. He accepted my friend request. I was so delighted when this message showed up on my phone. I rested my phone on my desk and went back to my work with his thoughts running on my mind. Though I didn't see him again that day, I had a feeling that maybe he wouldn't be suspicious. The day went off without any clue of him. And even on the following day, there wasn't anything different in his behaviour. Maybe he isn't thinking anything strange about all this. I rested my mind with this thought.

The next morning I woke up with a hope to find a message or at least a simple smile when we come face to face. But alas, he seemed way too normal. Nor did he try to utter a word or pass a smile, neither did I dare to. The day passed away. It was after a week or so when one day I was getting into our room listening to songs and he was coming out answering a call when we bumped into each other. Our foreheads were hit against each other like a slight rub before we stumbled and stood back. He was about to leave when I asked him to wait. He gave an awkward look like what happened, when I replied that "if we hit our head only once, we will get horns, we need to hit again". Listening to this first he gave a what the heck- kinda look, then burst out in laughter. He was about to leave when I held his face and gave a touched my head to his head and rushed back into my room. He was shocked but left in a minute.

I never knew this act of mine would result in such a manner. I never thought about this silly small act of mine would bring such a big change in my life. The very next minute, he completed his call, he came back into the room and kind of announced about my act and made fun of how stupid I am. This literally drove me crazy, seeing everyone commenting on their views on my level of stupidity. My anger turned to tears within moments and I sat on my chair shedding tears like a cry baby. Once he realised I was crying, he came to me apologising for making fun of me. I said it's ok. But he cracked some jokes and made me laugh before he left for work. This would remain one memorable moment of my life, I will never ever forget.

Things changed after this incident. Whenever he would cross the room I work in, he would stop by to see whether am still crying and would say "u crying again?". Gradually we started talking to each other and slowly we got closer. Now, I think we reached a point where I can call ourselves "friends". I finally found a friend in him. Now I can make him smile and see and adore that smile I loved from day one.

Yesterday in the morning, after I reached my workplace, we had a seminar on some work-related topic. As the seminar ended, everyone rushed out of the conference room to their cubicles, when I found a diary laid on the table. I went there and picked it up. I turned the first page in an attempt to know the name of the diary owner and return the same to them. I To my surprise, as I turned to the first page, I found a small envelope attached to the inside cover of the diary and over the envelope was written in bold "Crush- The reason behind my smile". I couldn't find the name of the diary owner, so I thought of opening the envelope out of curiosity. I was shocked at what I saw. It had a picture of mine and behind the picture was a heart symbol with an arrow. I was standing there with a diary in one hand and the picture in another when the door was suddenly opened. He came swiftly and grabbed the diary from my hand and was taken aback when he saw my picture in my other hand. He apologised and said he never meant to hurt me but didn't know how to confess, for which I replied "I Love You" too. When he read out the content over the envelope again, this time looking into my eyes, the thought of that smile I always admired was just for me, made me blush.

34

LOVE OF THIRTY DAYS

Day 1: (Monday)

35

Dear diary,

Today was my first day at college. I missed my school friends a lot. But I made some new friends at college too. Today we had orientation classes and college tour. This place seems nice and friendly. That was all about today. Oh, wait I forgot to mention him. Today after college, we were standing near the bus and discussing the day. Then I saw a boy, probably our senior staring at us. This seemed weird when I moved away from that group to another girl I met before in the class, and she told me that he was still looking at me. At first, I was frightened I don't know why, but later I ignored and thought maybe he was noticing in a casual way. Then we sat on the college bus and came back to the college hostel. This was all about today.

Day 2: (Tuesday)

Today at college, we were introduced with respective faculties and classes just began. We had an intro session where we students introduced ourselves in the class and our hobbies and schooling percentile. Then at lunch, I went to the cafeteria with some new friends. We ordered food and as I was taking back my meal to my table, I accidentally collided with him. The same senior I was talking about yesterday. He looked at me and asked "fresher?". "Yes", l replied with hesitation. He smiled and said "Varun, from CSE" and offered a handshake. I replied "Arohi, from CSE as well" and shook hands with him and joined my friends without looking back at him. Then I had food with Sara, Mishti, Swapna, and Ritika.

Day 3: (Wednesday)

At present, all branch students were made to sit together divided into two sections. Our classrooms are in different building other than from the department blocks. Once we complete our first year, we would be shifted to our department blocks. But there are places like the cafeteria, labs, library and bus stand where we have interaction with seniors.

Today, we had classes only in the morning. The second half of the day was spent on the ground playing sports. Our class boys were having a match with the seniors. There were girls of their class cheering them. And here we juniors don't know many by names, so we decided to cheer calling "the first year". It was a tough match of basketball. But juniors won over seniors. That felt so nice. But every time Varun made a goal, he would pass a smile to me. At first, it seemed like he smiled towards the audience. But after it got repeated a couple of times, I was sure he smiled at me. After the game was over, we got into our buses and came back to the hostel.

Day 4:(Thursday)

Today was just a casual day except for the fact that Swapna noticed yesterday's Varun's smiles after every goal. She was teasing me all day. But then I said it was nothing and changed the topic. I went to a stationary mart after my college with Swapna for purchasing some books and stationery. There we purchased the necessary things and were waiting at the billing counter when Varun walked straight to us. I was shocked to see him there. But then he said, "Hi" and Swapna waved her hand in a gesture of hi excitedly. I wonder whether this is just a coincidence or he is willingly following us.

Day 5 :(Friday)

Today was a long tiring day. We had continuous math classes for more than 2 hours. M1 is a subject that doesn't need any special adjective to describe it's horrifying. After the classes were done, we reached late to the bus stop to find the bus was already full. I was with Swapna standing on the bus with a tired face when I found Varun on the same bus. He got up from his place offering us a seat. This made Swapna poke me with her elbow and a smile. I made a teasing face but sat happily. This was the first time I was impressed with his act of care. Finally, when he was about to get down near his stop, he gave a small pat on my head in a gesture of goodbye and left. Unknowingly I gave a smile at him. I wonder if this makes him think am interested in him too.

Day 6 :(Saturday)

Today is Saturday. Our college principal planned a surprise for us. All first-year students were taken out to a nearby garden and a museum as a welcoming picnic to energize all of us. We all had great fun today. We clicked many pictures, went for boating and played games in the garden. While on the bus, we sang songs and celebrated this new phase of our lives. Then we were sent home a little early than the regular days.

Day 7: (Sunday)

Sunday vibes! Sleep, Eat, Repeat.

Day 8 :(Monday)

Today, I was in the library scanning all bookshelves for a book when he suddenly appeared from behind "what's up fresher? Bunking classes' right from the beginning?" he inquired. "It's our library class and am here for a book on computer architecture but couldn't find one", I replied. He suddenly held my arm and started pulling me by the hand towards the other side of the library and to a cornered shelf. I tried freeing my hand but he wouldn't let go. Then suddenly he gave a short push and I leaned on a bookshelf by my back. He came closer to me and placed a hand on the shelf towards my right as if blocking me from going to the right and leaned closer as if he was about to kiss. Startled I shut my eyes tightly and after a few seconds opened my eyes slowly to see him standing a foot away from me crossing his arms and a book in his left hand and a teasing smile on his face. When I opened my eyes, he gave a pat with that book on my head saying "silly you! Here's your book" and walked away smiling.

Even now at midnight, after so long from the moment this happened, I can still feel butterflies in my stomach, exactly the same way I felt in the morning.

Day 9 :(Tuesday)

Today I wasn't feeling much well so; I took leave and stayed at the hostel. I slept till noon then had some food and completed some college work. In the evening, I sat near the window in my room looking out and listening to songs when a text popped up on my mobile. It read 'Hi fresher'. I knew it was Varun but still acted like I didn't know it was him and texted back 'who is it?' Another message popped up 'I know u know it's me. Now just come down. I have something for u'. Now I was confused about what did he say and replied "what?" For which I got a reply "am waiting outside your hostel, come down and meet me". I replied, "I don't want to" and was trying to peep through my window to see if he really was here. He really did and he gave a call this time and asked me to come down just for 5 minutes. I said just for 5 minutes and tied my hairs into a bun and went down there. He was standing there leaning back on a car. The moment I went there, he asked me how I was, thanks to Swapna who told him that I caught a cold and was suffering from fever. Now, he brought me some medicines and gave them to me. He insisted me to take them and then I had to. Then we had a small talk and he left. I came back to my room. Though I don't like to admit this, I like the way he cares for me.

Day 10 :(Wednesday)

I woke up to a Good Morning text from Varun. Then I got ready for college. I came down my hostel building to find him waiting for me. Today we sat together by bus and were talking all the way. When we finally reached the college, he joined his friends and left and so did I. I don't want to but I feel I started liking his company. During lunch, Varun made sure to come by and pay a visit. He inquired if I was feeling good and left. When it was the last hour of class, there was some meeting held for faculty and we had no lecture. I went to sit in the library and read a novel I brought with me. When I got a call from Swapna. She asked me to come to the indoor games room. I went there to find Swapna was waiting for me along with Sara, Mishti and Ritika. They were looking so tensed and quiet. I was worried about what could have happened. I walked to them and enquired what was wrong. Sara came up saying "due to elections to be held in the next month, our class tests are proponed to last week of this month and we would be having extra classes from tomorrow to complete our syllabus on time". My heart sank down on hearing this. The first exam in the first year made us all feel nervous and tensed. But it's just a week in college and we are having extra classes? This is a not so fun situation. We all sat there planning revenge on people who said: "study just for these 2 years and then once you are in college, it's only fun and events". The day ended with vivid feelings and emotions.

Day 11: (Thursday)

The next morning, I found approx 10 miss calls from Varun. I don't remember when I dozed off last night worrying about my exams. I tried calling him, but he didn't answer my calls and I left for college. I tried calling him again, but it was again unanswered. I waited for him in the cafeteria at lunch, but he didn't turn out. In the evening after college, we had an extra class and we stayed late. It was already dark by the time our classes ended. And Sara had a doubt, so we stayed for a bit more than others. Since it was too late we were hungry and Sara proposed to go to a new cafe recently opened in the next street. As we reached there, the cafe was all decorated and colorful. We went inside to find no one over there, except for the staff. Maybe it was already their closing time I thought. We ordered some pasta and started clicking some pictures. Suddenly, the lights went off. There was darkness everywhere. Sarah turned on her mobile flash and asked me to accompany her to the restroom since it was too dark. It was after a few minutes that she came out and we opened the door to the cafe when suddenly the lights got lit. I could see Varun, his friend's jay, Mohan, Shyam and my friends, Mishti, Swapna, and Ritika. The cafe was all decorated with scented candles, flowers and balloons. And a cake was placed at the centre along with a flower bouquet and everyone else standing around the table while Varun walked to me and stood on his knees with a ring in one hand and another hand in a posture as if asking mine. Jay was shooting the whole time when finally

Varun proposed me and asked for my hand. I was surprised and shocked for a minute, then I replied 'yes' with tears rolling down my cheeks and hands trembling while reaching out for his. Oh my god! I can't believe this actually happened and now we are here together for real.

Day 12 :(Friday)

It was half-past seven when I woke up. I remembered last night and a smile kissed my face. I reached my hand out for my phone and I checked for calls or messages. Then I changed to my college outfit and was about to start for my college when I got a call from Varun. He came to pick me up. We were talking about different topics related to college, life etc all the way. It felt like we reached too soon than expected. After a few classes, it was our lunch. I went to the cafeteria to find him already waiting for me. He treated me like a princess. He pulled the chair for me to sit; he brought the food for me. After the break, we went back to our classes. In the evening, when it was time to get back home, he came to my class to offer a ride back home, which I accepted for. When we reached my place and I was about to leave, he called me back and leaned and planted a goodbye kiss on my cheek and left. This feels so nice to be around him.

Day 13: (Saturday)

48

Since everything was sorted between me and Varun now, I thought of concentrating on my tests to be held from Monday. Our class was on a mass bank today and we're doing combine studies with our groups. In the evening, Varun came after his college, and we went for a walk and discussed how my preparation going on and what we did the whole day is.

Day 14: (Sunday)

I don't remember how the day went off unknowingly with me studying all day and Varun went out with his family to attend a relative's wedding. The next week went in a swift with me busy with my exams and Varun at their relative's wedding.

Day 20: (Saturday)

Today we had our last test, after that we all classmates went out to party. We watched a movie, and then had dinner and then the party continued till late at night at a disco in the same mall. My phone was silent all this while and I missed calls from Varun. When I went back home, I saw he was constantly calling me for the past few hours. I thought it was already late and I would surely give him a call back in the morning.

Day 21: (Sunday)

Early the next morning, I called Varun as soon as I got up. But his phone was not reachable. I thought maybe he was busy and went back to my regular routine. I tried calling him every now and then in the day, but either his phone would be switched off, or he wouldn't just answer my call. I thought maybe he was upset with what had happened yesterday and decided to talk to him in person tomorrow.

Day 22: (Monday)

The morning, I went to college and directly went to Varun's class. But surprisingly he wasn't there. As for what I knew, Varun never came late but maybe he is today. During lunch, or even after college, I tried calling him or directly reaching out to him, but strangely nothing worked out. I felt disturbed all day; I couldn't concentrate on my classes or on any work. All I could think was just about him.

Day 26: (Friday)

It's been five days since I saw Varun or spoke to him properly. I wonder where he is from the past 4 days. I can't reach his phone or find him in college. I was wondering what happened suddenly when I got a message from him. It said, "This isn't working out between us. Let's breakup. Please don't message or call me anymore. Good Bye". After reading the text, I collapsed on my chair. It was quite devastating. I tried to call back again but his phone was switched out. I immediately went to his class and asked his friends about his whereabouts. But none had any clue. I went on to the terrace of the building and cried for an hour or two. Then I got a call from my roommate that my family is here. I was shocked to hear this and got back to my place as soon as possible. I got back to my room to watch that my mom was packing my bags. I was surprised. When inquired they told me to just keep silent and follow them back to our home. I couldn't speak out a word and did as they asked me to.

Day 27: (Saturday)

We reached home by noon. There were my grandparents waiting
for us. Dad asked me to freshen up, have some food and take
some rest. Later in the evening, I asked mom, what was
happening; she directly ignored me like there wasn't my
existence. I slowed sneaked to my grandparents' room and went
near my grandmother. She was sitting on bed knitting some
sweater. I went near her and asked softly that did she know what
was happening. She replied "you will get to know soon darling.
But tell me one thing, why are you looking so dull and
depressed? Is everything okay at college and with you?" I felt
like crying out loud that I was shattering inside after what Varun
has done, and speak out what all I was going through in the last
few days but smiled and said," I am fine mama, it's just some
stress related to studies and I was missing you all". She pulled me
closed and kept her wool and sweater aside, and placed my head
in her lap. She was combing my hairs with her hand and told me,
"You know your father loves you a lot, whatever he decides, and
it would be the best for you. Make sure you understand what I am
telling to you and follow your father's words for a better future".
I felt something suspicious is happening behind me in here, but
decided to wait till they unveil it by themselves.

Day 28 :(Sunday)

53

My mom woke me up in the morning and asked me to get ready as soon as possible as we will be going out for some shopping. Before I could ask anything, she replied, "Your father will be answering your questions in the car, now get ready first and come quickly". I got ready and when we were in the car driving towards the mall, I asked my father that why all of a sudden I was brought back home and now, we are shopping early in the morning. He replied sternly, "you are getting engaged day after tomorrow. Choose a nice dress and jewellery accordingly and remember I am not asking for your permission, I am informing this to you". He sounded like a south Indian movie actor but this was the first time of my life that I ever saw him so serious. For a moment I felt like the sky was crashing down all of a sudden on my head. First, it was Varun and now it's my father, I was totally lost in my thoughts and unknowingly we reached the place. As I lost all my senses, after all, that happened, my mom chooses everything by herself and we came back home. I didn't have any food and couldn't even sleep at night. My mind was all wandering about what is happening and I was like in a kind of shock all day.

Day 29: (Monday)

I made up my mind to tell dad about Varun, or at least tell him that I don't want to get married any soon. As I went to my dad's room and tried to speak out, he called me and said, "if you are here to talk about your engagement, then my answer is no, it can't be cancelled". I insisted I don't want to get married and want to study now and work in my dream company, for which he replied, "you are just getting engaged now. You can continue your studies and fulfill your dreams even after your engagement. We will do your marriage only when you complete your studies and tell us that you are ready to get married. Till then we won't' disturb you, but for now, get engaged without creating any scene". I held back my tears and ran to my room. I couldn't stop crying and fell asleep unknowingly. When I woke up, it was already evening and my grandma was by my side. She held my hands in between hers and said, "Remember what I said the other day? Your father loves you a lot, whatever he decides, it would be best for you. Now stop crying and be brave and pray for the best". I tried calling Varun for one last time to let him know what was happening and he surprisingly answered this time. I sobbed for a while and told him everything. All he said was, "if you really love me, do what your father asks you to" and hung up the call. Now I am left with no other choice, except listening to my dad.

Day 30: (Tuesday)

The house was all getting decorated and it's just 10:00 am now and I can already smell sweets and dishes cooked in the kitchen. All my relatives started coming and so did my friends. I wonder who called them. Then my mom saw me watching all this and asked me to get ready soon. I got dressed and was made to sit on the decorated chair placed on the stage like platform when my cousins and friends started dancing and enjoying. I was thinking how are these people that they aren't bothered a bit about what's happening inside me and are partying around. I was looking at everywhere down there from the chair when I suddenly saw Varun. I couldn't believe what he was doing here. He was coming towards me. I got nervous watching him come towards me. He directly sat on the chair next to me and started talking to me. I just got terrified about what dad will do to him if he saw Varun here. I was trying to make varun go back and leave this place but he wouldn't listen and all he would say is "let me see who your fiance is". I couldn't understand what he was doing and why all of a sudden he has to be here bothered to this extent when a week ago, he was the one who wanted us to break up. After asking him a couple of times, I pulled him by the hand and was about to take him down the stage when my dad came on the stage like out of the blue and questioned, "Where are you going?" I was out of words when a cousin of mine commented, "Ha, didi batao, jiju ko Kaha leke jaa rhe ho?" I got panicked and replied to dad, "he is a college friend of mine...", when my dad interrupted,

"I know everything. Varun came to me a week back and told me everything and asked for your hand in marriage. At first, I got angry and rejected, it was when he stopped talking to you. But he never complained about me to you or tried to elope with you and that was when I liked his nature and we both families planned this surprise engagement for you". I finally took a calm deep breath and the engagement ceremony took place well.

That's a different story that I got angry with Varun and stopped talking to him for a week for not letting me know this and made me go through all this. But in the end, we happily got together and promised our families to work on our career as a priority.

57.

LOVE AT THE AGE OF SIX

One fine morning, I was dressed well, and mom combed my hair and pinned a handkerchief to my shirt. She asked me to carry my new school bag and held my hand and walked me to the car. Then when we reached a place, a building named school. There were many kids around my age group walking around with their mom or dad. Finally, she took me to a room and asked me to greet a lady sitting across me on the table. I said good morning and she smiled and offered her hand for a handshake. She asked my name and I replied, "Shreya". She replied, "Welcome Shreya" and asked my mom to drop me to the class accompanied by a bhaiyya who came in running when that lady clicked on a switch that gives out sounds (which later mom told me as a calling bell). The class was a room full of desks and chairs and the walls were filled with paintings and children were sitting on the chairs and some of them were chattering, some laughing and some crying. A thin tall lady was saying something to them. Mom pulled me near and said that this lady is my teacher and I should behave well with her. Then I questioned was the earlier lady, my teacher too and she replied, no she is your school's principal. in the meantime, the teacher came and spoke something with mom whom I couldn't properly hear and I never bothered about. Then she shook hands with me and took me into the class and made me sit to a boy on the second bench. She clapped her hands and called out everyone and said they got a new friend and her name is Shreya and asked everyone to say hi to Shreya. They were a loud noise, of people saying "hi Shreya" involuntarily. I smiled and said "hi everyone". Then the school bell rang and everyone stood in their places and folded their hands and closed their eyes. We had a 5-minute prayer session that we sat back on our benches. All this while, I noticed the boy next to me was crying. I asked him what was the reason and he replied he was missing his mom and don't want to come to school but his mom sends him every day to school. I explained, "even I don't want to come here and leave my mom alone at home. But my mom said if I go to school and study well, I can get a good job and my mom and dad very well and can buy as many toys and chocolates as I want. And that's the reason why I agreed. Also, my mom made a deal that every day, if I am good at school, she would give me chocolate when I get back home". "Your mom is so sweet. My mom didn't make any such deal with me. I also want chocolate" and saying this, he started crying loudly. I was surprised and panicked maybe I would get into some danger and mom would not give me my chocolate or she would stop sending me to school. I closed his mouth with my hands and said," let's share my chocolate" and surprise he stopped crying and started smiling. When he noticed I was staring at him, he said his name is "Shreyansh". The day passed and I went back home. My mom gave me a bar of chocolates she promised and I kept it in my bag to share with Shreyansh the other day as I promised him.

The next morning when I went to school, the first thing I did was to share my chocolate with Shreyansh. As I was eating my half chocolate, he planted a kiss on my cheek and said thank you. I smiled and gave a slight slap on his shoulder. The school bell rang and the teacher came and the classes went on. in the recess time, when it's time for lunch, one of my two rotis fell down and

I was making a face, watching this Shreyansh shared his half roti with me. I ate happily. After lunch, he asked me for his thank-you kiss and I blushed. Later, we went to wash our hands near the washbasin when I looked here and there and noticed that no one was there and planted a kiss on his cheek. He gave a smile and shook hands with me and we called each other "friends". Days flew and we grew from class 1 to class 5 and from friends to best friends. We would go to school and come back home together. We would sit at lunch together and play games in the games period together. We heard people talking behind us out of jealousy but it never bothered us for our bond was stronger than any misunderstandings.

We were in class 6 when I got attacked by chickenpox and had to take rest and leave from school for 2 weeks. As it was the beginning of the new academic session, new students got enrolled in our class; one of them was "Priti". After I got cured properly. I went back to school to find Priti sitting beside Shreyansh, in my place. I asked her politely to change her seat as I was sitting with him from class 1, for which she refused. I got angry and pushed down her books and it was then when Shreyansh responded. Surprisingly, he shouted at me for behaving like that and asked me to sit with someone else as it was not a big deal and we would still be friends. That day at lunch, I waited for him on our same bench under the same tree during the whole lunch but he didn't turn out. And when the bell rang and I went back to class, I saw him walking back to class with Priti, hand in hand. When he saw me, he left her hand and came running to me and asked whether I had my lunch and I replied yes. As I was about to leave, my box slipped my hand and fell on the floor and the lid came out open. He saw that my tiffin was full and replied," I tried searching for you but couldn't find you, so I ate with Priti". I smiled and said, "We ate on the same bench for the last 5 years and you couldn't find me that am great", and I left. That night when I was at home and having dinner with my parents, I asked them to send me to my grandparents in Mumbai. I said I want to do my further schooling from there. At first, they took me lightly thinking I was just saying this normally but when I started crying and stood stubborn to move to, they had to agree.

The other day dad came to school with me and I wasn't in my school uniform as I went to collect my transfer certificate. A girl from my class saw me and inquired what happened? And I replied "am moving to Mumbai forever". She went to class and spread the same to everyone. in the meanwhile, principal called me and dad. We went in spoke to her, collected my transfer certificate and were walking back to the car when Shreyansh came running. He greeted dad Namaste and asked me why are you leaving all of a sudden? I replied, "I don't feel like I belong here. I feel suffocated in this place". And got into the car as Shreyansh was about to say something. Dad watched him and said, "Maybe he has something to say to you". I replied," there is nothing I need to hear from him anymore. Let's go". Shreyansh stood there with tears in his eyes all the time until the car turned away from his sight.

Moving from a city like Jaipur to a city like Mumbai is a very different thing. At first, I had to face many problems adjusting to the new lifestyle. But my anger on Shreyansh turned to be my motivation. Years passed and I completed schooling. I was about to get into a college. in the past few years, my anger for Shreyansh turned out to Love. I realised we were more than friends. I was with a hope that after schooling, I would go meet him, and say sorry and things would get back to normal. That summer vacation, after 6 years, I went back home, to Jaipur. I went to my old school, met many teachers, my old school friends but I couldn't find Shreyansh. waited for a couple of days and then went to his house, where he used to live earlier. it was locked. I went to the guard and inquired when he would come back. The guard replied," they left to Delhi a week ago for Shreyansh baba's college studies. They shifted to Delhi permanently." I asked if he had any number, or address of their whereabouts in Delhi for which he had the answer as "no". I cried for my bad luck that I missed him just by a week and after a few days, went back to Delhi for my college. I met new people, made new friends but no one could get special to me as Shreyansh did. Days passed and I completed my graduation too. But still, Shreyansh was in my heart and my mind.

I got a job offer from a company that had branches in Delhi, Mumbai and Bangalore. But I insisted to shift to Delhi with a hope to find Shreyansh. My parents wanted me to stay with the grandparents at Mumbai or come to them to Bangalore as dad got transferred to Bangalore in the last year. But again I won with the stubbornness and shifted to Delhi alone. My task would be like working at the office on weekdays and searching for Shreyansh on weekends. This continued for almost a year but there wasn't any positive response. I lost hope too.

One evening I was making coffee for myself when my phone rang. it was my dad. When I answered the call, he seemed panicked. He said, "your mom is sick Shreya. You need to come over as soon as possible". Saying this, he hung up the call. I booked tickets to the very next flight available and landed there by night. Dad said, "it's already too late. Go and take some rest. We can go and visit mom tomorrow at the hospital". That night I couldn't properly sleep and waiting for the morning. in the morning, dad took me to the hospital. Mom had been fighting cancer for the past few years, but both my mom and dad never let me know this as this could disturb me and I wouldn't do well at my grades. Now, mom is in her final stage and doctor's say; they couldn't help anymore. Now it's hardly a month or two or even days on the count. Hearing all this, I crashed to the floor and couldn't stop my tears. I regret that I left these people when I was in class6th just for my own ego and issues. Now even though I want to spend time with my mom, she has no time left for me. I wiped my tears and went to mom. She was lying on the bed weak and faintly. I called, "Maa". she slowly opened her eyes and saw me and asked me to sit and said, "nothing happened to me, dear. I will back home healthy and happy by evening. these doctors just exaggerate things. By the way, did your father give you your favourite laddoos I prepared for you? I know he forgot, wait I will call him and he called to dad". Dad came in. I stopped mom from saying anything and I said, "what could I do for you Maa?

is there anything that would make you happy?" She said," I wanted to see you get married. I always had dreams of watching you dressed like a beautiful bride and walking down the aisle. But I know you just started your career and wouldn't like to get married soon. But no worries, I will watch my darling in the bridal attire getting married from above". I immediately without a second thought said," Dad, I want to get married within this week. I will marry anyone whom you and mom for me but let's make this wish of mom fulfill as soon as possible". He understood how I felt and said," ok dear. I have a boy in my mind. He is my friend's son and works at ….." I interrupted my dad and said," yes I am okay with all those".

My wedding date was fixed and the shopping for clothes and other stuff happened like in a flash. Within no time, all the arrangements were made. Mom was wheel-chaired by the time my wedding date got neared.

The big DAY came. The rituals started and I kept close to mom all the time and she found happiness in dressing me up, dolling me and walking me to the wedding hall. Dad walked me down the aisle to the stage. There was standing a tall man in a black tuxedo waiting for me. He had a spark in his eyes and tease in his smile. His face seemed quite similar to me." What did dad say about him, his name?" I kept on thinking and trying to think of what was his name when the priest called out our names for "I do" rituals. And I heard him say "Shreya, Do u accept Shreyansh to be your husband…." I could only hear these lines and I looked at my parents with joyful tears in my eyes realizing this is the Shreyansh I have been waiting and searching for. My mom nodded with a smile and I replied," yes I do". Then it was Shreyansh's turn and he replied" Yes, I do" and passed a wink to me. This is the best time of my life. The love of my life, the one I have been waiting and longing for is finally and officially mine.

Signing off…
Miss Shreya,
Oops.
Mrs Shreyansh

66

RADHA, I LOVE YOU

It was a hot summer morning. I was busy in the kitchen helping my mom. She was teaching me to cook different types of dishes as in a few months they would get me married and daddy wanted me to learn all household chores before that. I prepared parathas for daddy today. He enjoyed eating them and said to mom, "Hema, your daughter is ready to get married now. She is cooking good". Mom passed a smile to me while I was preparing more. After cooking parathas, I helped mom wash clothes and do dishes. In the noon, I sat beside mom and started working on the saree that I stopped yesterday doing embroidery, while mom was taking a nap beside the radio. I was made to stop my schooling a year ago and was sent to a lady in our neighbourhood who teaches stitching, weaving and embroidery. As I had been a fast learner since my childhood, I completed my 6-month course in 3 months and had started making clothes, embroidery and weaving sweaters for my relatives and Radha. Radha is my only best friend, I had ever since I was 1. Their parents shifted to our neighbourhood when we were 1 and since then we are each other's best friends. Radha was married last month and my dad wanted me to get married soon too. I always wanted to study and learn more in life. I was topper in my class but as I turned 13, dad wanted me to learn cooking and tailoring. Since I loved to study, I never had enough time or attention to pay towards cooking or anything. That was when dad decided to drop me out form school and to send me to cooking and tailoring classes. In the beginning, I cried a lot and wouldn't eat properly but they never bothered and forced me to attend those classes. So, I finally gave up and started learning them and finding my happiness in them.

I was lost in my lost when suddenly mom called my name and asked me to prepare tea for her. After serving tea to mom, I went to the terrace and brought the dried clothes, folded them neatly and dusted the house and cut vegetables and prepared everything for making dinner. Then my younger brother 'Vijay' came home back from school. I gave him some snacks and he went out to play. I prepared dinner and dad came home. While having dinner, dad said to mom, that on the next day, his friend will be bringing a suitor for me. He asked mom to dress me up early in the morning and to prepare sweets and snacks for the same. Mom stayed up all night to prepare snacks and sweets but asked me to take proper sleep or else, my face would look dull in the morning. I tried sleeping but thoughts kept running in my mind. The other day Radha came from her Sasural to meet her parents, she told me how life changes after marriage and I never would love living such life. Thinking about how to survive all those strange looks and living with completely new people, I felt nervous and afraid too. Unknowingly I fell asleep.

In the morning, as usual, I woke up at 4, broomed the house, mopped everything and made rangoli. Then I took bath, got ready and was about to enter the kitchen to prepare breakfast when mom called me from behind and said, "Today I have prepared the breakfast. You go get ready, look pretty" and left. I felt like am I a showpiece to look beautiful and ready to be purchased? Why should only a girl have to leave her house after marriage, why wouldn't boys do the same? Why can't I study more? I kept thinking and was wondering when dad called out, "Hema, they are here. Come fast". For the next few minutes, I could hear indefinite greetings and chatters and laugh. Then suddenly everything went silent. Mom came to take me. She asked me to carry a tray of tea. "Carrying a saree wasn't enough that I need to hold this tray too" my inner voice felt like screaming. But I kept a constant small smile on my face as my mom directed me to. I served tea and sat on the carpet with my face lowered as an act of shy. Dad and the other uncles who were with him discussed something among themselves and dad hinted mom to take me back into the room and I was headed back to my room. I was made to sit there for an hour or so and then they left. Dad came back into the house saying, they liked our girl. They would be sending the pandit tomorrow for fixing dates and soon she will no more be ours. Mom came in running and kissed me on the forehead and said," My girl, you already grew up and are about to fly far away from us" and started crying when dad said, "stop crying at such happy hour and come we need to make plans for the marriage preparations". With this, they left me in solitude. I changed into my casual clothes and sat near the window wondering.

The other day pandit came home and fixed the marriage dates for the next week. Mom kept saying, "it is too early" but dad insisted, "we will manage". I thought," was I that burdensome?". Everyone got busy in the marriage preparations. Even Vijay took leave from school to attend our relatives and cousins. Day by day our home got filled with more and more relatives. Every day a new ritual continued. Within a flash, it was my marriage day. They made me sit in front of the mirror for the past few hours. Suddenly someone shouted, the groom is here with his baraat and everyone left the room running. I kept sitting there looking at my reflection in the mirror. I felt suffocated in this 6-yard saree, and

all this Mehendi and jewellery. I got angered and was about to
pull out my necklace when my mom came in. she was surprised
to see me in such a frustrated mood. As I saw her, I tried acting
normal. Then she sat near me and explained that in a girls life,
getting married and bearing children is the ultimate motive and
completeness of a woman. She explained to me the importance of
marriage and how much she and dad love me and how I should
behave in my Sasural such that I don't my parents in a shameful
situation. I kept listening silently to what she had to say and
replied with a nod every now and then.

The ceremony started and ended after an hour or so. Then the
Vidaai part started as we were to catch a train that shouldn't be
missed. This was the first time I saw my dad with teary eyes
while mom sobbed hugging me. Suddenly I felt some energy of
maturity and responsibility. We sat in a car and reached the
station. Then we started by train. I sat near the window and my
husband was sitting next to me, followed by his dad and mom.
Opposite to us was his sister, brother and aunt.

We reached my new home by the evening. Then I was asked to
follow some other rituals and finally, I got an opportunity at night
to take some rest in my sister-in-law's room. Then around 11 pm,
my sister in law and mother in law came along with other ladies
and helped me to get ready for another puja. After the puja was
completed, I was let to my husband's room. I sat on the bed
nervous. After about 10 mins approximately he came. He locked
the door and dragged a chair to the bed. He spoke to me for the

first time. He said, "I have just completed my graduation. I got a job in a company but was willing to pursue my post-graduation". My father didn't agree to the same and I fought with him and left home and went to Bangalore to pursue my dreams. It's been three months and then one day, I got a letter from my dad which said, "Dear Ravi, your mother is seriously ill. She needs to have a look at you. Even the doctors have informed that nothing can be done now". After reading that letter, I came home as soon as possible. But to my surprise, it was all a trap to bring me back home. They organised and made preparations for my marriage against my will and also forced me to marry you, or else they will commit suicide. I am forced into this marriage. I never wanted to marry you. Don't expect anything from my behalf". He left the room after completing his version of explanation even without a look for my expressions. I cried myself to sleep. Early the next morning, I heard a knock on the door. I opened and found Ravi standing outside. He rushed inside and closed the door again. He said, "I forgot to inform you that whatever we discussed last night, should remain between us. You shouldn't let anyone know what is happening between us". I was wondering, "how could you speaking all by yourself to me be called a discussion". My thoughts were interrupted when he shouted, "you understand?". And I nodded my head in agreement. We stayed there for the next 3 days and then moved to Bangalore.

Bangalore is a big city, a place that is calm and beautiful. I hoped to sort things with Ravi and lead a happy life. But things didn't turn out the way I thought they would. Ravi behaved completely like a stranger to me. We hardly speak to each other and forget about going out for dinner or date. Few months passed and things gradually started changing. Though I don't find any love in his eyes for me, at least we started communicating. Few more months passed and it was our marriage anniversary. I asked him to come home early and prepared his favourite dish for dinner. After having dinner, I asked him for the first time to take me out shopping and surprisingly he agreed. I brought a saree for myself and a watch for him. We came back home and from the next morning, things continued to be the same as usual. After a few more months, I realised I conceived and shared the same with him. He was not very happy to hear the news but wasn't sad at the same time. After nine months, I gave birth to a cute little boy. We named him "Rakesh". After 2 more years, I conceived again and this time it was a baby girl. We named her "Reena".

With time, our love started fading again even before it bloomed properly. Rakesh was five and Reema was three when I went to Rakesh's school for his admission and while returning back met with an accident when Reema got injured. This was the first time Ravi lifted his hand on me. He wouldn't listen that It was an accident. But the thing that made me happy is that I saw how much he loved our children. From that day, he frequently started slapping or beating me for every small or big reason. Years passed and I got used to all this. Rakesh and were always good at academics and sports. It was Rakesh's 12th when he passed with flying colours. His father wanted him to join IIT and pursue engineering. He did the same while Reema topped in her class 10 exams and chose Medicine field. After completing his graduation, Rakesh joined a software company in Pune and started earning well. While Reema completed her MBBS and started her practise in Pune itself.

One morning, Ravi was reading a newspaper and I was preparing his breakfast when the doorbell rang. I opened the door and to my surprise, it was Rakesh with a girl. Both had garlands around their neck and suitcases in their hands. I understood what happened and called Ravi. He asked them to get in and enquired the reason behind taking such a drastic step. For which they replied that they feared rejection from both the families but also couldn't think of living without each other. Ravi called Shweta's (daughters-in-law) parents and informed them about this. They came over to our house in the evening and after discussing, both the families decided to organise a reception for the new couple and celebrate their marriage. When Reema heard the news, she was delighted and overwhelmed by her brother. She came home to attend her brother's reception unaware of her father's planning to get her married.

For a moment, I saw myself in my daughter. I tried to protest Ravi from doing this but it didn't help anything. Reema was engaged to Suraj, son of Ravi's friend at work, on the same day Rakesh's reception was arranged. Within a month, she was married to Suraj and sent to her in-laws.

Everything was happy at the beginning but things didn't work very great later. Rakesh loved Shweta a lot and always cared for her. He used to take her out weekly, cook for her at times she felt down, support her with her career etc. and Shweta too balanced her professional and personal life carefully. She takes out enough time for Rakesh and family as well. But Reema wasn't that lucky. Suraj was not at all supportive towards her career and she had to stop her work. She was made to sit at home and look after the house and her in-laws. He wouldn't bother whether she is well or not or even had food or not. The next year, it was our marriage anniversary when both of our children came here to meet us along with their families. It was then when Ravi realised what was happening with his daughter and daughter in law.

He decided to talk to Suraj and asked him about the reason behind ill-treating Reema. He gave an example of how Rakesh takes care of Shweta and how much they love each other and support each other in personal and professional life. For which Suraj gave a reply that left us dumbstruck. "Why are you feeling that bad suddenly? I treat your daughter in the exact same way you treat my mother-in-law. I took you as an example and started treating my wife the way you treat yours". On hearing this, Ravi was shocked. Rakesh added, "That's a true dad. What is wrong in that. If you can treat mom like that, why can Suraj treat sister like that?". After hearing this, Ravi stumbled in shock. I held him by the shoulder and made him sit on a chair. I said," I will bring water for you" and was about to leave when he held my hand and apologized, "I always kept in mind that this marriage was against my will and I never bothered to understand your perspective. I was so lost in my own disappointment that I never realised your hidden pain and love for me. Please forgive me Radha". This was the first time in my life that Ravi called me by my name. He always used to call me, 'Aye, Oye, Hey' etc. He turned back and plucked a rose from the vase on the table and bent down on knees and proposed me, "Radha, I love you. Will, you be my beloved? Let's restart our love life from the beginning". Tears ran down my eyes and I said, "Yes, I love you too". We hugged and then

Suraj and Reema came up and said, they planned this situation willingly to make Ravi realise his mistake and they are living a happy life together, respecting and loving each other. Thus, my story too had a happy and a lovely ending.

www.ingramcontent.com/pod-product-compliance
Lightning Source LLC
Chambersburg PA
CBHW031221160726
47992CB00006B/2837